P9-DXG-949

Library and Archives Canada Cataloguing in Publication

Cole, Kathryn author
Fifteen dollars and thirty-five cents : a story about choices /
by Kathryn Cole ; illustrated by Qin Leng.

(I'm a great little kid series)
Co-published by: Boost Child & Youth Advocacy Centre.
ISBN 978-1-927583-82-1 (bound)

1. Honesty—Juvenile fiction. I. Leng, Qin, illustrator
II. Boost Child & Youth Advocacy Centre, publisher III. Title.

PS8605.O4353F54 2015 jC813'.6 C2015-903294-6

Illustrations by Qin Leng
Design by Melissa Kaita
Printed and bound in China

Boost Child & Youth Advocacy Centre gratefully acknowledges the generous support of Rogers Communications for funding the development and publication of the Prevention Program Series. Rogers Communications is an important partner in our efforts to prevent abuse and violence in children's lives.

Second Story Press gratefully acknowledges the support of the Ontario Arts Council and the Canada Council for the Arts for our publishing program. We acknowledge the financial support of the Government of Canada through the Canada Book Fund.

Published by
Second Story Press
20 Maud Street, Suite 401
Toronto, Ontario, Canada
M5V 2M5
www.secondstorypress.ca

Fifteen Dollars and Thirty-five Cents

A story about choices

written by Kathryn Cole
illustrated by Qin Leng

Second Story Press

A flash of silver on the ground caught Joseph's eye. Then a gust of wind sent some dry leaves swirling away from him. When Joseph looked more closely, he saw two coins sparkling in the sun. And those "leaves" were really five-dollar bills – three of them!

"Look!" he said to Devon. "Money!" He chased the bills and scooped up the coins – a quarter and a dime. "I'm rich!" He counted out the money. "Fifteen dollars and thirty-five cents."

Devon wasn't sure about the math, but he knew that Joseph was holding a lot of money. "Wow," he said. "What are you going to do with it?"

"I don't know yet," Joseph said. "I might spend some and keep some."

"Maybe you should take it to the office," Devon said. "Somebody must have lost it right here in the schoolyard."

"No way," Joseph said. "Finders keepers, I always say."

"And losers weepers," Devon mumbled to himself.

Joseph and Devon were good buddies. They did everything together. Devon could see how happy his friend was with the money, but something didn't feel right when Joseph stuffed the bills into his pocket. Devon tried again.

"Think about it, Joseph," he said. "Somebody lost that money. Maybe someone we know. Let's take it to the office. We should try to find out whose it is."

"It's *mine* now. You just wish you were the one who found it," Joseph said. "Tell you what. I'll give you five dollars, and then we'll both have some money."

Devon wanted the five dollars, and he didn't want to lose his friend. He thought about it. *Maybe we don't know who lost the money. Maybe the stranger who lost it is really rich and won't miss it. Maybe the kind, rich stranger even left it here just so some little kid could find it. Maybe this is just good luck. There's nothing wrong with good luck.*

Devon was just about to take the money when Lin and Claire passed them. They were walking slowly and looking down at the ground. Lin was sniffling.

"Did you see that?" asked Devon. "They are looking for something. I bet it's the—"

Just then, the bell rang and morning recess was over. Everyone hurried into the school. Joseph pretended he hadn't seen the girls, but Devon knew he had.

During reading, Lin looked very sad. Ms. Crosby asked her if she felt all right. When Lin didn't answer, Claire spoke up. "She's upset because she lost the money she had for her mother's birthday present. She saved her allowance for weeks and weeks, but it fell out of her pocket."

"Or got stolen," Dee-Dee said. Devon looked at Joseph. Joseph looked at the floor.

"Anyway," Claire continued, "Lin and her big brother were going to buy a present after school, but now her mother won't get anything. Lin lost fifteen dollars and thirty-five cents."

"You better make her a really nice card," Dee-Dee said.

Ms. Crosby spoke up. "Maybe someone honest found it," she said. "Devon, will you be Lin's partner and go to the office with her to see if the money has been turned in?"

Devon got up slowly. Joseph dropped his eraser as his friend stood. He bent down beside Devon to pick it up. "Don't tell," Joseph hissed. "They'll think I took it."

Devon kept walking. *Losers weepers,* he thought, looking at Lin's tear-stained face.

Of course, the money wasn't in the office, it was in Joseph's pocket. Devon didn't know what to do. He was Joseph's friend, but Lin was also his friend. Should he tell on one friend to help the other? What if everyone *did* think Joseph had stolen the money? The longer this went on, the more it would look like Joseph was a thief.

By lunchtime, Devon looked like he might cry too. Ms. Crosby asked him to stay for a minute after the bell rang.

Joseph gave Devon a worried look. "I'll save you a seat in the lunchroom, Dev," he said, "because good friends always stick together, right?"

When they were alone, Ms. Crosby sat down beside Devon. "You seem almost as upset about Lin's money as she is, Devon. Is there anything you'd like to tell me?"

"Well, I do want to tell you…and I don't want to tell you," said Devon. His throat was beginning to sting. "That's my problem. I don't have the money, if that's what you mean."

Ms. Crosby looked right at Devon. "No, that's not what I meant." She smiled a kind smile and waited. The silence made Devon want to say more. And once he got started he couldn't stop.

"What would you do if you had a good friend, and that friend didn't take the money, but he found it instead? What if the friend said 'Finders keepers,' and he was going to share some of the money with you? And what would you do if you had another friend who lost the money and she was really, really sad, and you felt sorry for both friends, and you didn't want to tattle, and—"

"Take a deep breath, Devon," said Ms. Crosby. "I think I see the problem. And do you know what else I think? I think the question is, what would *you* want someone to do if it was *your* money that was lost?"

Devon shrugged. "I'd want them to give it back, as long as they didn't get into trouble for finding it."

"You have made a good choice by telling me this. Maybe you can help your friend make a good choice too." Ms. Crosby got up and went to her desk. She picked up a white envelope and handed it to Devon. "This might be helpful. Tell your friend it's a hint."

Devon wasn't sure what the hint was, but he took the envelope. As he was leaving, Ms. Crosby said, "By the way, Devon, I'm going for lunch now too, so if you need anything, I won't be back for a while."

"Did you tell on me?" Joseph wanted to know as soon as Devon sat down beside him.

"No," Devon said. "But you need to find a way to give Lin her money back."

"How do we know it really belongs to her?"

"Joseph! It's fifteen dollars and thirty-five cents. That's how much Lin had for her mom's present. Lin was looking for it right where you found it. It's her money, and you know it." Devon took a deep breath. "I'm your friend, but if you don't give it back, I will have to tell. You choose."

Joseph sighed. “I don’t even want the money anymore. But what if Lin thinks I took it? I should have said something sooner. Now it looks…”

Devon remembered the envelope that was still in his hand. Suddenly, he knew what to do. “This is a hint,” he said, holding it out to Joseph. “And here is another hint. Our classroom is empty right now.”

Devon left Joseph alone to think.

That afternoon there was an envelope sitting on Lin's desk. Inside were three bills and two coins – fifteen dollars and thirty-five cents. Everyone cheered and Lin clapped her hands. She felt like the happiest person in the world… but she wasn't.

Devon was happier. Ms. Crosby was happier.
And Joseph was the happiest of all.
The smile on his face said so.

For Grown-ups

About Making Choices

Decision-making is the ability to choose between different options. When making choices, children need to consider the positive and negative consequences of each option. Helping children to stop and think about all of their options and consider what impact each would have – on themselves and others – can develop their ability to make healthy choices. Children can practice this skill at any age. They develop confidence in their ability to make healthy decisions when they know they can ask for help and support.

Parents can support their children in learning how to make positive choices:

- **Provide opportunities for choice:** Give your children the chance to make age-appropriate decisions every day.
- **Express confidence in their ability:** Let your children know that you have faith in their ability to make reasonable choices.
- **Consider others:** Consider your children's feelings when you make decisions and they will learn to consider others in their decision-making.
- **Respect the choices of others:** Show children that you respect the choices of others by accepting their decisions, as long as no one's well-being is jeopardized.
- **Consider different points of view:** Show children that you value what others say, but have the confidence to make decisions that are right for you.